SPARTAN WARRIORS

by Luis Sepahban

The Child's World®

Published by The Child's World
1980 Lookout Drive • Mankato, MN 56003-1705
800-599-READ • www.childsworld.com

ACKNOWLEDGMENTS
The Child's World®: Mary Berendes, Publishing Director
Red Line Editorial: Editorial direction
The Design Lab: Design
Amnet: Production
Content Consultant: Gary Eddy, PhD, Professor of English,
Winona State University
Design elements: iStockphoto
Photographs ©: Public Domain, cover, 27, 30 (middle);
Shutterstock Images, 4, 30 (top); National Geographic
Society/Corbis, 7, 18; iStockphoto, 9, 12; iStock/Thinkstock,
14, 19, 30 (bottom); DK Images, 17; Bettmann/Corbis, 21,
22; North Wind Picture Archives, 26

ISBN 9781631437601
LCCN 2014945427

Printed in the United States of America
Mankato, MN
November, 2014
PA02246

ABOUT THE AUTHOR

Lois Sepahban has written several books for children, covering science, history, biography, and fiction topics. She lives in Kentucky with her husband and two children.

TABLE OF CONTENTS

King Leonidas led an army of Spartan and Greek warriors against the Persians.

CHAPTER ONE

THE BATTLE OF THERMOPYLAE

Sparta was a powerful **city-state** in ancient Greece. Around 500 BC, Sparta and other Greek city-states were in danger. The mighty Persian Empire wanted to expand westward. The Persian army slowly conquered one Greek settlement after another. For a while, the conquered Greeks lived in peace under Persian rule. But they were not happy with their new government.

In 480 BC, all the Greek city-states united to fight against the Persians. King Leonidas led the Spartan military. Spartan warriors were brave and strong. King Leonidas was a warrior, too.

In the early fall, Persian ships were spotted off the east coast of Greece in the Aegean Sea. The Greek warriors split into two main groups. One group would battle the Persians at sea. King Leonidas led the other group. It would battle the Persians on land.

Some Persian troops camped along the coast of Greece. They planned to cross the mountains through a narrow pass. They would then march from there to Athens, another powerful city-state.

The Greeks wanted to stop the Persian army at the pass. If the Persians made it through, they would be able to easily attack Athens. The pass was not the only way through the mountains. There were smaller trails that herders used, too. But the pass was the only way a large army could get through. So King Leonidas commanded his warriors to block the pass.

King Leonidas had an army of more than 6,000 soldiers on land. His army included Spartan warriors and warriors from other city-states. But they faced a much larger army. There were more than 100,000 Persian soldiers camped near the pass.

For four days, the two armies faced each other without fighting. King Leonidas had fewer warriors, but they would not leave the pass. The Persian army waited. They hoped their larger numbers would scare away the Greeks. But the Greek warriors were not frightened.

On the fifth day, the Persian army grew tired of waiting. They attacked the Greeks with arrows. Then they sent out waves of warriors. King Leonidas and his men fought the Persian army. Night came and King Leonidas's army still blocked the pass. On the sixth day, the Persian army attacked again. King Leonidas and his army did not give up. Then a Greek **traitor** told the Persians about a small path

King Leonidas sent most of his warriors away before the final battle.

King Leonidas had left unguarded. Going through the path would allow the Persians to surround King Leonidas and his men.

The Persian army began surrounding the Greeks. Soon King Leonidas saw what the Persians were doing. He sent most of his army to safety before they were completely surrounded. Those Greek soldiers needed to get away to protect Athens.

King Leonidas decided to hold the pass with 300 Spartan warriors. They would protect the rest of the Greek army as it escaped. Other Greek warriors volunteered to stay behind with the Spartans. They included 700 Thespians from Thespiae and 400 Thebans from Thebes. King Leonidas had 1,400 warriors total to face the entire Persian army. King Leonidas and his men knew that they would not survive the battle.

At dawn on the seventh day, the Persian army attacked. King Leonidas and his men fought hard. But they were surrounded. They fought to the last man. By the end of the day, the Persians had won.

King Leonidas and his warriors died at the pass at the Battle of Thermopylae. The Greeks lost to the

Many warriors died at the Battle of Thermopylae.

Persians. But the brave Spartan warriors who died there held off the Persian army. It gave the other Greek warriors time to save Athens.

WARRIOR VALUES

Spartan values emphasized strength and courage. When a Spartan man was 20, he was old enough to be a warrior. He joined a warrior's club where he learned to depend on the other warriors. In battle, this same group of warriors fought side by side. Each warrior used his shield to protect the warrior on his left. Spartan warriors believed that running from battle was a great shame.

ANOTHER VIEW
THESPIAN WARRIORS

The Thespian warriors who stayed behind at Thermopylae were not as well trained as the Spartan warriors. Still, they fought alongside the 300 Spartan warriors to the last man. Why do you think the Thespian warriors stayed to fight beside the Spartans?

CHAPTER TWO

THE BIRTH OF SPARTA

Sparta was a small city-state on the large Peloponnesian **peninsula** of modern-day Greece. Sparta was in a valley surrounded by mountains with a river that flowed all year. Its fertile soil was good for crops. The valley also had plenty of pasture for sheep.

The Spartans controlled all the land near Sparta, but they were not content. They wanted to conquer lands beyond the mountains. For nearly 500 years, from the tenth to the fifth century BC, the Spartans fought for control of the entire peninsula.

It was during this time of war that the Spartans developed their military system. Greek warriors were called *hoplites*. They got their name from their shield, which was called a *hoplon*. In most of Greece, soldiers

A later artist imagines the market square of Sparta.

were farmers or herders. They became soldiers when
it was time to go to war. But Sparta was always at war.
They tried to conquer neighbors or fought with slaves
who wanted their freedom. So Sparta needed *hoplites*
who were full-time warriors.

Spartans created laws about the roles of Spartan men. They were not be farmers, craftsmen, or fishermen. Those jobs were for slaves and conquered peoples. Instead, free Spartan men were warriors. The laws said Spartan warriors could not live with their families. Instead, they had to live in buildings with other warriors. Their whole lives were focused on training for battle.

ANOTHER VIEW
SPARTAN WOMEN

Strength and courage were important for Spartan men and women. Spartan girls exercised and ate healthy food just like Spartan boys. In other Greek city-states, girls were not allowed outside to exercise. They were married around age 13 or 14. In Sparta, girls were not allowed to marry until age 20. Spartan women did not battle in wars, but they were skilled fighters. And while Spartan men were at war, Spartan women took care of their property and their husband's property. Unlike other Greek women, Spartan women were taught reading, writing, and math. How do you think other Greek women felt about the life of a Spartan woman?

THE PELOPONNESE

The Peloponnese is a peninsula in southern Greece. It is almost completely surrounded by the Mediterranean Sea. The city-state of Sparta was in the southern part of the Peloponnese. Other major city-states on the peninsula included Corinth, Argos, and Megalopolis.

Sparta (in red) was on the peninsula of the Peloponnese.

CHAPTER THREE

ARMOR AND WEAPONS

When a Spartan warrior went into battle, he carried a *hoplon* on his left arm. The *hoplon* was a round shield that was curved in at the edges. A *hoplon* weighed about 16 pounds (7 kg). It was a little more than 3 feet (1 m) in diameter. It was made with a wood frame covered with bronze. The *hoplon* was the most important part of a *hoplite's* armor. A Spartan man without a shield could not be a warrior. And a Spartan man was only given **citizenship** if he could fight. So the shield became a symbol of citizenship for Spartan men. It was often passed down from father to son.

Most Spartan weapons and armor were made of bronze. Bronze is a hard metal that is difficult to pierce through.

Spartan shields had designs carved into them, such as a monster's head or a Greek symbol. The carvings were meant to frighten Sparta's enemies. When enemies saw the shields, they knew the mighty Spartan army was coming.

A *hoplite* warrior carried a long spear into battle. The spear was 8 to 10 feet (2 to 3 m) long. It was the warrior's main weapon. The head of the spear was made of bronze and barbed or leaf-shaped. The handle of the spear was made of wood. The end of the spear handle was pointed so it could be used as a weapon if the spearhead broke off.

Spartan warriors trained with other weapons, too. They used arrows, slings, and swords. In battle, a *hoplite's* sword hung from his waist. He used the sword if he lost his spear. Arrows and slings were used mainly for practice. They were not common in Spartan battles.

In addition to their shields, Spartan warriors wore crested helmets. The crest was meant to look frightening. Most crests stretched from the front of the helmet to the back. Sometimes the crests went from side to side.

Spears were important weapons to Spartan warriors.

Hoplite warriors wore short-sleeved tunics. Over the tunics, they wore a cuirass. A cuirass is a type of armor that covers a warrior's chest, back, and sides. Spartan warriors also wore metal and leather guards for their arms, shins, and knees.

Training Spartan Warriors

A Spartan boy lived at home with his mother until he was seven years old. At seven, he went to live with other boys in **barracks**. The boy's training was meant to make him strong and teach him to obey orders. During training, boys were often beaten by men or older boys. Sometimes, the boys were not given enough food to eat. Then, they had to steal food. If they were caught stealing food, they were punished. Their punishment was not for stealing, but for being caught. Spartan warriors thought that boys who could steal without being caught were clever.

A Spartan boy hides a stolen fox under his robe.

ANOTHER VIEW
CHILDHOOD

The duty of Spartan children was to become strong men and women. As soon as a Spartan baby was born, it was judged. If a baby was weak, it was taken to a mountain and left to die. If a baby was strong, it was given back to its mother. Spartan boys and girls learned to read, write, and do math. They also learned music and dancing. Exercise was important for all Spartan children. While boys left their family home at age seven to learn to be warriors, girls continued to live at home to learn from their mothers. What do you think childhood was like for Spartan boys and girls?

Spartan boys grew up to be warriors.

CHAPTER FOUR

BATTLE TACTICS

The Spartan military invented a battle formation called a *phalanx*. In a *phalanx*, *hoplites* lined up in rows and columns to make a rectangle. The men stood close to each other, shoulder to shoulder. In battle, they moved together. Each warrior carried his shield on his left arm and his spear in his right hand. With his shield raised, the *hoplite* protected himself and the warrior to his left. An individual warrior could not stand against a *phalanx*. Even warriors on horseback were easily defeated by a *phalanx*.

Because the armor and weapons *hoplites* carried were heavy, they were not able to march long distances. They also had difficulty fighting on sloped ground. But on flat

Warriors fight in a *phalanx* formation.

ground, a well-trained *hoplite* army could be terrifying to its enemies.

What set Spartan warriors apart from other Greek warriors was their upbringing. Spartan soldiers were trained from birth to never give up. Their duty was to die for Sparta. Surrender in battle was shameful. It was even worse to survive a battle if the Spartan army was

Spartan warriors fought fiercely in battle.

defeated. Spartans believed that if one warrior was left, the battle should continue.

By the time a Spartan warrior went to his first battle, he was well trained to fight. He never dropped out of the *phalanx*. He followed orders. He did not back down from the enemy.

When not in battle, Spartan warriors practiced military **drills**. They stood in a different *phalanx* depending on the type of battle. One *phalanx* was shaped like an open wedge. The warriors formed a triangle, which pointed toward the enemy. Another *phalanx* formed a slanted angle. They also fought in a crescent shape, which curved toward the enemy. Hoplites fought in these different groupings depending on the location of the battle. For example, in the tight pass at Thermopylae, *hoplites* formed a wedge *phalanx*.

In a *phalanx*, soldiers slowly lowered their long spears as they marched into battle. But the first several rows of *hoplites* kept their spears straight out. The sharp tips were ready to meet their enemies.

Spartan Religion

Ancient Greeks, including the Spartans, worshipped many gods and goddesses. Archaeologists uncovered two temples in Sparta for the goddesses Athena and Artemis. These two temples show what was important to the Spartans. Athena was the goddess of war and Artemis was the goddess of the hunt.

Another View
Spartan Slaves

At the bottom of Spartan society were slaves. Slaves were captives who had been defeated by the Spartans. They could be beaten or killed for no reason. They were not allowed to become *hoplites*. They did not have a voice in the government. Slaves were also used to work on farms. Slaves could be bought or sold, and they were treated badly. How do you think slaves felt about how they were treated in Sparta?

CHAPTER FIVE

MAJOR SPARTAN BATTLES

By 650 BC, Sparta was one of the most powerful city-states in Greece. Sparta built its power by battling neighbors and taking over their lands. Another powerful city-state was Athens. Sparta and Athens united against invaders, such as the Persians. But they did not always get along.

Around 480 BC, Sparta and Athens united to fight against the Persians. The Greek city-states were under attack by the Persian Empire. The Persian army had defeated the Spartans at Thermopylae before. But the Persian army had been defeated in many battles, too. It was losing its strength. The Spartan army had lost many warriors when King Leonidas and his army

The Greeks battled against the Persians at Plataea.

were killed. But the Spartans knew that all the Persian troops were in Plataea, in central Greece.

The Spartans prepared to defeat the Persians in Plataea. Spartan warriors lined up in their *phalanx* formation. They met a Persian army made up of **cavalry** and small groups of foot soldiers. The Persian cavalry charged at full speed at the *phalanx*. But the Spartans' *phalanx* held. When the Persian cavalry and foot soldiers raced into the *phalanx*, the long spears brought them down. At the Battle of Plataea, the Spartans destroyed the rest of the Persian land army in Greece.

Next, the Greeks needed to defeat the remainder of the Persian navy. Later in 479 BC, they did so. The Persian navy retreated across the Aegean Sea. Then, the Greek navy attacked at Mycale. Mycale was a settlement in modern-day Turkey. After this Greek victory, the Persians left the Greek city-states alone.

A *hoplite* battles against a Persian warrior.

Sparta and Athens were able to work together to fight off the Persians. But their friendship did not last long. Both city-states wanted to be the most powerful in Greece. Soon, their argument became a war.

Across Greece, different city-states took sides in this argument between Sparta and Athens. In 431 BC, **allies** of Sparta attacked Plataea, an ally of Athens. Then Sparta invaded the countryside of Athens. That angered the Athenians. So the Athenians used their navy to **blockade** city-states allied with Sparta. The Peloponnesian War had begun.

27

For more than ten years, this pattern of fighting continued. Spartan *hoplites* invaded Athenian allies on land. And the Athenian navy blockaded the allies of Sparta by sea. Around 421 BC, Sparta and Athens called a **truce**. But it did not last long. In 420 BC, they were back to war.

For years, there was no clear winner. In 418 BC, Sparta and Athens fought in Mantinea, and Athens was defeated. And in 410 BC, Athens and Sparta fought again. This time the battle was at sea. Athens won.

The Peloponnesian War finally ended when the Spartan army blockaded the Athenians from 405 to 404 BC. The Athenians eventually surrendered. The Spartan army forced them to take down the walls around their city. The Athenians also gave up most of their ships and goods. The Peloponnesian War had lasted 27 years.

The Spartans were warriors who spent their lives protecting Sparta. They fiercely defended Sparta from its enemies.

The Decline of Sparta

Sparta proved that its military was the most powerful in Greece when it defeated Athens. But the Spartan victory did not last for very long. After many years of war, the Spartan army was shrinking. In Sparta, only Spartans could join the military. Because the Spartan military was weaker, people who had been conquered by Sparta were able to grow stronger. Sparta's neighbors and slaves fought for their freedom. Thirty years after the end of the Peloponnesian War, Sparta was back to the size of a city-state.

Another View
The People of Athens

In times of peace, Athens and Sparta had little in common. The two city-states were opposites. Art and poetry were important to Athenians. Spartans believed war and strength were important. Spartans did not trust outsiders. Athenians welcomed outsiders. Spartans did not use coins or money. Athenians wanted everyone to use them. Spartans gave women many freedoms and rights, but Athenians did not. How do you think different values affected the two city-states' relationship?

TIMELINE

500
BC
Sparta and other Greek city-states are in danger of being invaded by the Persian Empire.

480
BC
Greek city-states unite to fight against the Persians.

480
BC
The Battle of Thermopylae occurs. The Spartans lose to the Persians.

479
BC
The Greek navy attacks the Persians at Mycale. The Greeks win.

431
BC
Allies of Sparta attack Plataea, an ally of Athens.

431-404
BC
The Peloponnesian War occurs between Sparta and Athens. Sparta eventually wins.

GLOSSARY

allies (AL-lyes) Allies are people or groups who join together for a common purpose, such as to fight a war. Allies of Sparta attacked Plataea, an ally of Athens.

barracks (BA-ruhks) Barracks are one or more buildings where soldiers live. At seven, boys went to live in barracks.

blockade (blok-ADE) A blockade is the closing off of an area so that people and supplies may not enter or leave. Athenians used their navy to blockade allies of Sparta.

cavalry (KAV-uhl-ree) Cavalry are soldiers who ride on horseback. The Persian army had cavalry and foot soldiers.

citizenship (SIT-uh-zuhn-ship) Citizenship is the rights and duties that come with being a citizen of a country. A Spartan man was only given citizenship if he could fight.

city-state (SIT ee state) A city-state is part of an empire with a central city and surrounding area. Sparta was a powerful city-state in ancient Greece.

drills (DRILZ) Drills are actions performed over and over again in order to learn how to do something. Spartan warriors practiced military drills.

peninsula (puh-NIN-suh-luh) A peninsula is a piece of land that sticks out from a larger land mass and is almost surrounded by water. Spartans fought for control of the entire peninsula.

traitor (TRAY-tur) A traitor is someone who helps an enemy and betrays his country. A Greek traitor told the Persians about a small unguarded path.

truce (TROOSS) A truce is a temporary promise to stop fighting. Around 421 BC, Sparta and Athens called a truce.

TO LEARN MORE

BOOKS

DiPrimio, Pete. *Ancient Sparta*. Hockessin, DE:
Mitchell Lane Publishers, 2013.

Green, John. *Sparta! Warriors of the Ancient World*.
New York: Dover Publications, 2013.

Park, Louise, and Timothy Love. *The Spartan Hoplites*.
New York: Marshall Cavendish Benchmark, 2010.

WEB SITES

Visit our Web site for links about Spartan warriors:
childsworld.com/links

Note to Parents, Teachers, and Librarians: We routinely verify our Web links to make sure they are safe and active sites. So encourage your readers to check them out!

INDEX